STAR WARS®

JEDI ACADEMY

by *New York Times* bestselling author
Jeffrey Brown

Scholastic Inc.

Thanks are due to many people for making this book possible:
Rex, Sam, Rick, and everyone else at Scholastic; J.W. Rinzler, Leland,
Joanne, Carol, and everyone at Lucasfilm; Marc Gerald, Chris Staros,
Brett Warnock, Steve Mockus, my family and friends, and everyone
else who has supported me by reading my books. Thank you!

www.starwars.com

Scholastic Children's Books
An imprint of Scholastic Ltd
Euston House, 24 Eversholt Street
London, NW1 1DB, UK
Registered office: Westfield Road, Southam, Warwickshire, CV47 0RA
SCHOLASTIC and associated logos are trademarks and/or registered
trademarks of Scholastic Inc.

First published in the US by Scholastic Inc, 2013
First published in the UK by Scholastic Ltd, 2013

TRADE: ISBN 978 1407 13870 1
NON-TRADE: ISBN 978 1407 13951 7

A CIP catalogue record for this book is available from the British Library.

Printed and bound by CPI Group (UK) Ltd, Croydon, CR0 4YY
Papers used by Scholastic Children's Books are made from wood
grown in sustainable forests.

1 3 5 7 9 10 8 6 4 2

www.scholastic.co.uk/zone

A long time ago in a galaxy far, far away....

There was a boy named Roan Novachez (that's me) who was destined to attend Pilot Academy Middle School and become the GREATEST star pilot in the GALAXY. Until everything went TOTALLY and COMPLETELY WRONG...

this is the face I used to make before this story started (Mom calls it my "nice face")

me... after everything goes wrong

Mom, did my letter from *Pilot Academy Middle School* come?

Not yet. I'm sure it'll come soon.

I can't wait... Davin said his first year at Pilot Academy was AWESOME.

Well, until then, you still need to get your chores done in the garden.

Oh, man, garden work is lame!

At least I won't have to go to Tatooine Agriculture Academy. I can't wait to fly in space!

My first comic strip! ↲

staR pilot
BY ROAM age 5

the smuglers ar attacking

oh no!

i'll get you guys

BOOM

you win a Medal!

Davin, Dad, and me

Roan

ANNUAL
STAR
PILOT
SIMULATION
CONTEST
2nd
PLACE

Dav at Pilot Academy

Oliver and Mom

Roan   T-16

9

Hey Ro,

Congratulations on finishing with primary school. I'll bet you're looking forward to the summer off. And then I'll bet you'll be here at Pilot Academy before you know it. Right now we're getting to fly these new prototype starships. It's not as good as your drawings, but here's a picture of what they kind of look like:

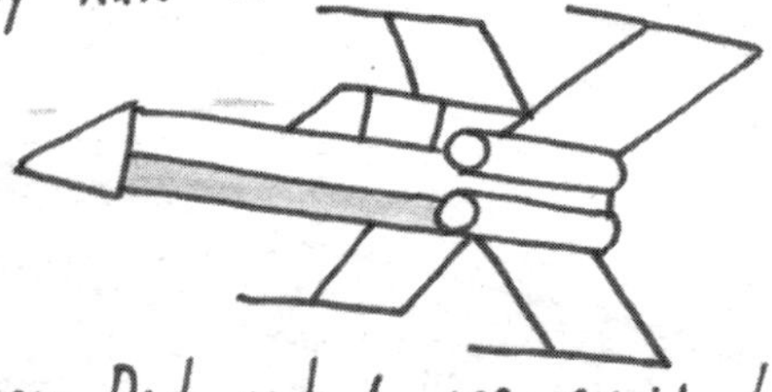

Anyway, Dad and I are excited to get you flying in some real starships soon!
– Dav (your brother, remember?)
P.S. Say hi to Mom and Ollie for me!

...and what's cool is I know I'll get in because of me, not because my dad's a pilot or my brother's at the Academy...

Guys, look!

Jax and I got our acceptance letters for Pilot Academy!

Did you get yours, Roan?

Um... no.

Congratulations, guys!

To: Roan Novachez
RE: Your recent
application

Dear Roan,
Thank you for your application
to Pilot Academy Middle School.
After reviewing your grades,
test scores, extracurricular
activities, letters of recommendation,
and personal essay, however, we
will have to <u>deny</u> your
admittance to the Academy
at this time. Although nearly
all of the applicants are
accepted to the Academy, a
small number of students are
rejected for various reasons.
We wish you all the best as
you begin this very exciting
new phase in your education!
 Best of Luck,
 Senator Blagotine

OFFICIAL USE ONLY	RECOMMENDED ALTERNATE SCHOOL:
	Tatooine Agriculture Academy

PILOT SCHOOL	VS.	PLANT SCHOOL
- Grandpa, Dad, and Davin all pilots		- I'll be stuck on Tatooine for rest of my life
- get to fly latest starships		- will need to spend more time washing dirt out of clothes
- air-conditioned cockpits		- will get sick of eating vegetables
- get to travel all over galaxy		- have to shovel bantha fertilizer
- wear really cool flight suits		- have to work alone a lot
- have wingmen to fly with		- have to stare at tiny patches of dirt for hours
- get to see planets from outer space		- sand gets in underwear all the time
- can listen to music while flying		- sweat will get on comic books during lunch break
- taking off is coolest feeling ever		

MY LIFE IS OVER!

DUODAY (worst Duoday ever)

So, Mom keeps telling me that this isn't the end of the world but it totally, definitely, absolutely is! Hold on, I'm going to shut my door and scream as loud as I can...

It's okay!

It's not the end of the world!

It's not so bad!

It's not a big deal!

why don't you write about it in your journal?

Okay, I'm back. I don't feel any better, though. I've never wanted to be anything but a starfighter pilot, except when I was four and I wanted to be a garbage speeder truck pilot. I don't even know <u>why</u> I can't go to Pilot Academy! And now I'm going to have to tell Dad and Davin, and they're totally going to be disappointed in me. When Reg and Jax find out, they're going to think something's wrong with me. It's like the ~~unverse~~ universe won't let me forget that I'm not going to be a pilot.

Roan!

Roan fly!

No, OLLIE. ROAN <u>NO</u> FLY.

Like, the same day I got my rejection letter, I got the new issue of Yuzzum's Quarterly Catalogue of Starship Technology.

I couldn't read the articles because I was so upset... I didn't even look at the pictures. I should cancel my subscription. And I should get ready for Tatooine Agriculture Academy, because that's my only other option now. Why would they even want me to go to plant School? This is what happened to the power couplers on the moisture vaporators after I worked on them for science and technology class:

Before Roan!

After Roan.

Oh, well, I guess it doesn't matter now. I'm doomed.

DOOMED.→

To: Roan Novachez
RE: Jedi Academy

Dear Roan,

Recently, your application to Pilot Academy Middle School came to the attention of Master Yoda at the Coruscant Jedi Academy. On his behalf, I would like to invite you to attend Jedi Academy this coming school year. Please find attached a brochure with your schedule, travel details, other information, and twenty pages of paperwork to fill out.

May the Force be with you,

PRINCIPAL MAR

Strong in you, the Force is - Jedi, you may be. Much potential, you have. Good to teach you, it will be!
- Master Yoda

PENTADAY

Well, I know where I'm going to school now: Jedi Academy. I guess it's okay. I know the Jedi get to use some kind of laser sword, which sounds pretty cool, although Mom mumbled something about safety. I don't know when Jedi use those swords, because I think they're diplomats or peacekeepers mostly. I was talking to Jax and Reg, and they said I must be lying, there was no way I got into Jedi Academy, because you only get chosen for Jedi training when you're a toddler. So I showed them the papers. Then they laughed and said I'm probably going to be in a class with babies. Anyway, it's on a planet called Coruscant, which is really far away:

← Tatooine   Coruscant →

It doesn't matter, though, because Mom already sent in my paperwork and I leave next week.
At least I don't have to go to Plant School.

Roan Plant!

WELCOME TO JEDI ACADEMY

Located on the teeming metropolis planet Coruscant, Jedi Academy is the galaxy's premier training facility for Jedi Knights. This state-of-the-art complex has everything necessary for the most complete Jedi training available, with the best and most promising young students learning at the highest levels.

JEDI ACADEMY F.A.Q.

WHAT IS A JEDI?

A Jedi is a diplomat warrior who fights for peace and justice across the galaxy.

WHAT TOOLS DO THE JEDI USE?

The Jedi uses a lightsaber - a kind of sword with a blade made of pure energy - and the Force.

WHAT IS THE FORCE?

The Force is an invisible energy field created by all living things. The Force gives a Jedi his power, allowing him to do extraordinary things, like moving objects with his mind.

WILL STUDENTS LEARN "JEDI MIND TRICKS"?

Jedi mind tricks are a way of using the Force to influence the thoughts and decisions of other sentient beings. Beginning students will not yet be instructed in mind tricks.

WHAT ABOUT THE DARK SIDE OF THE FORCE?

The dark side is an aspect of the Force arising from negative emotions such as anger or hatred. Students at Jedi Academy will be taught how to resist the dark side.

WHO WILL BE TEACHING?

Jedi Academy's faculty includes veteran Jedi, notably Master Yoda, who has hundreds of years of experience.

MEET THE FACULTY OF JEDI ACADEMY

PRINCIPAL MAR
Science, Philosophy

MASTER YODA
Using the Force

MRS. PILTON
Math, History

KITMUM
Physical Education

MR. GARFIELD
Lightsabers,
Home Economics

LIBRARIAN LACKBAR
Literature, Art

RW-22
Student Advisor

T-P3O
Tutor
(2nd Semester)

Students will live full-time at the Jedi Academy campus, where they will be instructed by actual Jedi Knights with real-world experience, in a full range of subjects — galactic history, science, lightsaber dueling, math, politics, art, writing, and using the Force.

Students will enjoy trying new and unusual meals from all over the galaxy in the Jedi Temple cafeteria.

Lifelong friendships will be formed on intergalactic field trips to star systems across the Republic for a culturally well-rounded education.

HEY ROAN—
MOM SAYS YOU'RE REALLY DIS-
APPOINTED ABOUT NOT GETTING
INTO PILOT ACADEMY, BUT I'M STILL
PROUD OF YOU — GETTING INTO JEDI
ACADEMY IS A BIG HONOR! I
THINK YOU'LL LEARN A LOT MORE
THAN YOU EXPECT, AND YOU'LL
HAVE A TON OF FUN — ESPECIALLY
IF YOU'RE LEARNING HOW TO USE
THE FORCE. YOU CAN ALWAYS
TRY AGAIN TO GET INTO PILOT
ACADEMY NEXT YEAR, BUT
GIVE THIS A TRY FIRST AND
SEE HOW IT GOES.
                    LOVE, DAD

P.S. HERE'S A PATCH LIKE THE ONE
I WEAR ON MY FLIGHT SUIT. JUST
REMEMBER I STILL BELIEVE IN
YOU.

I think I'm lost...

Hey! Hey, you!

I'm Pasha. You're the new kid, right? What's your name?

I'm Roan.

Hey, new kid!

This is Bill.

BEEP BO BLEEP!

RW-22 says "Welcome to Jedi Academy."

Watch it!

Who's that?

It's a new kid.

BUMP!

26

28

Thoughts About Master Yoda

2 swords

battle scar

What I first imagined Yoda would be like

2 feet tall

smiles a lot

green

what Yoda is actually like

6 feet tall

tough

looks like a puppet

— Everything up-mixed, says he. Backwards, he talks.

very, very wrinkly

I can't understand what he says half the time. He IS seven hundred years old. Maybe he was easier to understand two hundred years ago?

Heh Heh Heh!

LOTS of ear hair

Hm?

Hmmm

Approximately 10 L.P.M. (laughs per minute)

15 H.P.M. (Hmmms per minute)

* May actually be teaching instead of being full-time Jedi because he's going kind of senile?

STUDENT: ROAN NOVACHEZ

LEVEL: PADAWAN | SEMESTER: ONE

HOMEROOM: MASTER YODA

CLASS SCHEDULE

0730-0850: BASIC LIFTING WITH THE FORCE
MASTER YODA WILL TEACH STUDENTS TO LIFT THINGS
WITH THE FORCE, INCLUDING ROCKS, DROIDS, AND BOXES.

0900-0950: GALACTIC HISTORY
MRS. PILTON WILL TELL STUDENTS HOW THE REPUBLIC
WAS FORMED, WHERE JEDI COME FROM, AND MORE.

1000-1050: ALGEBRA
MRS. PILTON WILL INSTRUCT STUDENTS IN USING
ADVANCED MATH EQUATIONS THEY WILL DEFINITELY
USE LATER IN LIFE.

1100-1150: SCIENCE
PRINCIPAL MAR WILL LEAD STUDENTS IN CONDUCTING
NUMEROUS EXPERIMENTS USING THE SCIENTIFIC
METHOD.

1200-1300: LUNCH BREAK

1300-1350: ARTS AND LITERATURE
LIBRARIAN LACKBAR WILL INTRODUCE STUDENTS TO
ESSENTIAL WORKS OF LITERATURE AND ART FROM
ACROSS THE GALAXY.

1400-1450: INTRO. TO LIGHTSABER CONSTRUCTION
MR. GARFIELD WILL TEACH STUDENTS HOW TO
BUILD THEIR OWN LIGHTSABERS.

1500-1550: PHYSICAL EDUCATION
KITMUM WILL KEEP STUDENTS IN SHAPE WITH
A VARIETY OF RIGOROUS ATHLETIC EXERCISES.

Wow, the halls are empty! I must be the first one getting to class today!

Late, you are...already begun, class has.

Oh, no! I had my watch set to Tatooine time!

MONODAY

So, I've only been here two days and I can already tell I don't fit in here. Literally. Even the souvenir Jedi Academy t-shirt I got was size extra, extra small. It seems like most of the students here are nice, at least, but they've all been ~~studying~~ studying the Force since they were little and I don't always know what they're talking about. I guess I always thought "the Force" was something we just said — you know, "May the Force Be With You" or "Good Luck" or "See You Later." But apparently the Force is an actual force. Like gravity. Except you can use it. Or Jedi can. I don't know if I'll ever be able to... the other kids say we spend part of each morning just "feeling the Force." I think that'll be all of us sitting around staring at the floor or something...

can't... breathe

I don't feel any— wait! Was that the Force?

No.

I will get to do lightsaber training, which will probably be the only fun part of this school.

Of course, my professor for that class is Mr. Garfield, who I met at orientation. I think he already 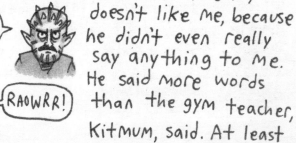 doesn't like me, because he didn't even really say anything to me. He said more words than the gym teacher, Kitmum, said. At least what I could understand, because she's a Wookiee. I can't remember the rest of the teachers' names, because I was already feeling overwhelmed. For now I'm going to hang out in my dorm room. It has a window, but the view isn't very interesting.

HOMEWORK ASSIGNMENT

STUDENT NAME: _Roan_ 18/20 A

DATE DUE: _next Quadday_

QUESTION ONE: Where does a Jedi's strength flow from and what does a Jedi use that for?

the Force ✓

knowledge and defense ✓

QUESTION TWO: Name three things a Jedi should beware of leading to the dark side?

1. anger ✓   2. ~~impatience~~ fear ✓

3. hate   ok- aggression

QUESTION THREE: How does a Jedi accomplish his or her goals?
A. Try   B. Try Not   (C. Do)   D. Do Not
E. None of the above ✓

QUESTION FOUR: What are the five core precepts of the Jedi Code?
1. knowledge, not ignorance   2. Harmony, not chaos   3. Peace, not emotion ✓
4. Serenity, not passion ✓   (5.) -1

TRIDAY

Well, I thought I finally sensed the Force last week. I started to feel light-headed and weird. From what I'm told, I started talking nonsense and then passed out. I woke up an hour later in a bacta tank (pretty cool, except being in my underwear). The medical droid told me I hadn't been eating enough or getting enough sleep. So I wasn't feeling the Force, I was just hungry and tired, which is totally not my fault. I'm still getting used to the cafeteria, because it serves the WEIRDEST food. Roasted tentacles?! Yuck. I finally tried more of the food. It's really not that bad if you're hungry enough. It's also hard to sleep, there's so much going on. I feel like I'm lost half the time. I AM lost half the time. Trying to find your way around the Jedi Temple is like trying to find your way around the Mos Eisley spaceport when you don't know what a spaceport is! When I get lost I look for someone I recognize and follow them...

that was my lunch

hop!

Cyrus and Cronah are in the same classes as me, so I tried following them around, until they started looking at me funny. Everyone knows way more than me, they've all had Jedi training

Why is the new kid following us?

for practically their whole lives. And I'm the only one from Tatooine, another reason I should be at Pilot Academy. Anyway, most of the work has been easy enough, except feeling the Force. Everyone has advice:

Find your happy place!
(didn't work)

Don't worry so much, give it time.
(still doesn't tell me HOW to do it)

Egon just stared at me. (At least he was staring at me sympathetically.)

So, last weekend some of the kids were going to see a holomovie and asked if I wanted ~~too~~ to go. I said I wasn't feeling well (which they believed after my passing-out incident), but really I was just relieved that I could be by myself and draw some comics. So I was alone in my room, sitting there with my journal, thinking about nothing in particular, when it happened:

Everything felt different, but the same... I think I've ALWAYS felt the Force, but I never realized that's what I was feeling!

Ro-

Sorry I haven't written in a while, we were on a training exercise in the Hoth system. You should be glad you aren't in Pilot Academy, we spent two weeks freezing on an ice planet! I was talking to the guys here about you going to Jedi Academy and they were actually all pretty impressed. Not to put any pressure on you, but I guess it's a big deal. You'll get to do some cool stuff there.

Don't let it go to your head, though, I'll still be a pilot before you're a Jedi!

-Day

P.S. The guys say I should let you know that "Jedi mind tricks" don't work on older brothers!

41

Remember to feel the Force!

Basic Lifting with the Force

1. clear your mind (except thinking about object you want to lift?)
2. use Force to lift object*

<u>TIPS</u>

↑ Yes

→ NO

*size does not make difference

Jedi do not use Force for simple convenience but Padawans should ~~try~~ (try not) <u>practice</u> using Force to turn on TV, make dinner, clean room

HOMEWORK: should be able to lift book from floor to table using only Force by next week

holomail

FROM: master_yoda_642
TO: Padawan Class Group
SUBJECT: Important Field Trip Information

OPTIONS
◀ REPLY
▶ FORWARD
▢ PRINT
⬤ POST TO HOLOBOOK

WHEN: WEEK SEVEN
WHERE: THE PLANET KASHYYYK
PURPOSE: To study Wookiee culture and technology, and various Kashyyyk ecosystems. Students' horizons will be broadened.

ACTIVITIES: Students will observe an official meeting of the Wookiee Council, tour Wookiee neighborhood settlements, and camp in forests of wroshyr trees to study native flora.

NOTES: Although students will be accompanied by several Jedi chaperones, they will be traveling through areas inhabited by katarns and webweavers, which are known to prey on small creatures.

CHAPERONES: Master Yoda, Kitmum, and RW-22

ITEMS TO BRING: Notebook and pen, holocamera, hiking boots, Wookiee Translation Manual, extra socks, snacks, water bottle, sense of adventure

DUODAY

We're back from Kashyyyk and I was going to put some photos from the trip in here, but I can't find my holocamera anywhere. I checked all my bags and everything. So somewhere on Kashyyyk there's a holocamera full of photos of me standing in front of stuff. I guess I'll just draw what I saw anyway.

Here's the Wookiee settlement ⟶ where we started out. Our first

activity was to watch the Wookiee Council in action, which I was expecting to be fun because Wookiees are like huge, furry monsters. But it was BORING. I guess Wookiees are very civilized, although they do wave their arms and growl a lot. Kitmum was translating for us, but that just meant she growled, too. At least we had her as a guide to show us around. When it was time to leave we had to wake Cronah up, because he fell asleep (and drooled on his shirt). Ronald took a lot of notes, though. I think he wants to run for student council president. So maybe watching the Wookiee Council will be worth it.

I have to say Kashyyyk is an amazing planet. My favorite part of the trip was camping. The trees were huge! We spent a big part of the morning packing everything on our bantha.

Yeah, they have banthas on Kashyyyk, just like on Tatooine! ...

They also have all kinds of strange creatures, which Yoda kept warning us about. It's hard to know how serious he was because he'd always laugh when he was talking about them...

Aware of predators, you must be! Heh Heh Heh!

Yoda

katarn

webweaver

48

We hiked out to the campsite and then got to explore from there. It started off bad, because Gaiana got really mad at me for something that was totally an accident. In fact, she didn't talk to me much the whole rest of the trip.

This is amazing!

Bend!

WHACK!

Gaiana, are you okay?

Geez, Roan!

I, uh—I'm sorry—

(I make that face a lot lately)

I felt kind of embarrassed after that so I explored on my own. We were supposed to meet back at camp at 1600, but when we did, Pasha was missing! RW-22 wasn't any help to search because he can't roll through the forest very well, so Yoda had us split up into search teams.

I'm glad we made it back before dark...

Why? Because it would be so hard to see?

No, because of the Ghost Wookiee!

The Ghost Wookiee is the spirit of an angry Wookiee who haunts the forests of Kashyyyk, looking for unsuspecting travelers to crush in its massive arms!

What? It's just a story, I'm kidding with you guys.

URR?

Uh...

AAIEEEEEEE!

Run for your lives!

RAORRR?

"scratch scratch"

ANNOUNCEMENTS!

JOIN
The Holochess Club!

Meet in Room 304

LOOKING FOR:
· Writers · Artists ·
· Photographers ·
Work for the Jedi
Temple's best
newspaper
*receive 3 class
extra credits

Don't forget—
Deadline to
run for student
council is:
Next Hexaday

Please recycle your
holocontainers!

LIGHTSABER PRACTICE
SQUAD begins meeting
after Gym Class.
DON'T BE LATE!
(supervised by
Mr. Garfield)

VISITING
PROFESSOR
LECTURE
Albert the Hutt
"On the Physics
of the Force"
Quadday
@1200

INSIDE YOUR LIGHTSABER

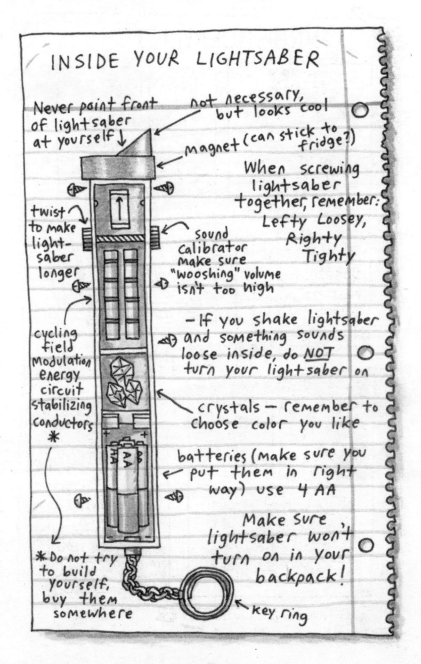

Never point front of lightsaber at yourself ↓

not necessary, but looks cool

magnet (can stick to fridge?)

When screwing lightsaber together, remember: Lefty Loosey, Righty Tighty

twist to make lightsaber longer

sound Calibrator make sure "wooshing" volume isn't too high

— If you shake lightsaber and something sounds loose inside, do NOT turn your lightsaber on

cycling field modulation energy circuit stabilizing conductors *

crystals — remember to choose color you like

batteries (make sure you put them in right way) use 4 AA

AA

Make sure lightsaber won't turn on in your backpack!

* Do not try to build yourself, buy them somewhere

key ring

All right, connect the stabilizer, and then we'll test your lightsabers.

I better not see anyone without safety goggles on!

click

Buzzzzzzzzzzz

click

Buzzzzzzzzzz

Click

Buzzzzzzzzzz

click

BzzzzzzTTtkkk

Can I switch lab partners?

Hey little bro—
Remember how you used to draw those
Ewok Pilot comics? We had an
exercise near Endor, so I was able
to get you some photos of real Ewoks.
Maybe you can use them to draw some
new comics for the school newspaper
or something? Anyway, I didn't learn too
much about Ewoks that you didn't
already know — they're short and
furry, say things like "Yub Yub" and "Ee
choya!" and use spears and clubs
for hunting. And live in trees.
...unds like you're settling
...riends — it's good,

TRIDAY

It's been an okay week so far. I've started working on "Ewok Pilot" comics for the Padawan Observer, and I got an "A" on my essay about the economic effects of the Cron supernova on galactic trade routes. This week we've all been working on our science fair projects. It seems like everyone is doing something Force-related... Bill has an environmental impact study on Jedi using the Force near rivers. Gaiana's using the Force to make tastier cough syrup. I can't even use the Force! At least not consistently. Cronah says ~~accidently~~ accidentally lifting pencils doesn't count. I was going to do a starfighter project, but Cronah and Cyrus are and said I was copying them. It'd be easier to think of something if I was home, here there's so much going on and it's hard to focus. So I guess there are advantages to places that are boring most of the time.

Since I couldn't figure out what I should do for my project, Pasha helped me brainstorm and I decided to make a baking soda volcano. I know that sounds pretty simple, but I ended up doing research about the volcanic planet Mustafar, and for my working model I included actual details of molten rock and liquefied minerals with information about how the planet's crust affects the magmatic activity.

Yoda's advice on the Jedi scientific method:

Only SOMETIMES must a Jedi clear his mind of questions!

Pasha and I ended up helping each other out on our projects. He needed someone to take the readings while he ran tests for his increased lightsaber crystal efficiency prototype (basically I just had to write down numbers). After that Pasha helped me paint some of the models for my volcano. Both of our projects turned out pretty good. I'm definitely going to get an "A" on my experiment!

Hmmm... much like a real volcano, this was!

Geez, Roan, I'm sorry... not much left of your project, huh?

No... all I found is this one tiny piece.

This is an exact replica of the TechnoUnion processing plant used to mine the rare ores of volcanoes on Mustafar.

Really? It looks like an old candy wrapper.

Oh. You're right, it is just an old candy wrapper.

The Padawan Observer

EDITED BY THE STUDENTS OF JEDI ACADEMY · VOL. MXII #7

CORUSCANT ACADEMY SCIENCE FAIR ENDS WITH BANG

This year's science fair ended with a bang-literally, thanks to Padawan Roan Novachez's malfunctioning Mustafar Baking Soda Volcano experiment. Master Yoda did not believe the accident to have been caused by "misapplication of the Force." Whatever the cause, Roan's volcano exploded, spraying students and faculty with a variety of baking materials.

Shi-Fara won first place at the science fair when her droid managed to clean up the entire mess in fifteen minutes without breaking anything else. Second place went to Egon Reich for his Force-powered Perpetual Motion Machine, despite the fact that the invention stopped running shortly after the end of the competition. (continued on page 2)

INSIDE:

(continued on page 2)

HEXADAY

Since I can still only lift tiny things with the Force, Bill offered to help me work on it this past weekend, and brought RW-22 over to my room. Bill sat there, concentrated for a moment, and then RW-22 floated right up into the air. Bill said it helps him to imagine RW-22 having rocket-booster feet. That sounded kind of silly, but considering my lack of success, I figured it was worth trying. So I stared, stuck out my hand, and focused on feeling the Force while imagining little rocket-booster feet on RW-22. RW-22 didn't budge, though. He just started beeping and whistling and spinning his head. Even Bill didn't know what RW-22 was saying, but it wasn't good. We got RW-22 calmed down and tried again. This time, RW-22 did move — not in the air, he just rolled away down the hall. He stopped and turned to give me one more annoyed beep. I don't know what I did wrong, but RW-22 was fine the next time I saw him. Maybe he erased the whole incident from his memory banks...

BEEP
BO
BOOP
BLEEP!

Art and Literature-Librarian Lackbar
Important artworks from Galactic Art History

*need to know these for <u>test</u>

The Mona Jedi
- the woman in this painting has a mysterious smile that is like the mystery of the Force

The Jedi Thinker
- this sculpture expresses the focus and concentration needed to use the Force

The Persistance of Hyperspace

Tatooine Gothic
- a portrait of simple farmers that contrasts with Naboo Royalty

HEY ROAN- I'M GOING TO RUN FOR PRES. OF STUDENT COUNCIL. DO YOU THINK YOU COULD MAKE SOME POSTERS FOR ME? -BILL

Poster Ideas

Why is this such a big deal to everyone? I need to come up with more ideas...

HEY ROAN - THANKS FOR MAKING THESE POSTERS FOR ME, THEY'RE TURNING OUT GREAT! YOUR SUPPORT MEANS A LOT TO ME!
— BILL

A *Nice* guy for *Nice* times

NOBODY LIKES GETTING BILLS. VOTE FOR RONALD.

ROAN - since you're making such good posters for Bill, you'll make some for me, too, right? Make one of me standing on Bill. →
— RONALD

- "Better Bald than Ronald"
- "Don't Vote Wrongald"
- "Bill-ding a better Jedi Academy"

charm. Ambition. Experience. RONALD.

VOTE BILL

A VOICE YOU CAN LISTEN TO, WHO LISTENS TO YOU

"Bad Change Is Bad, Re-Elect Ronald"

Do you think these campaign ads are getting a bit too negative?

Maybe.

DON'T VOTE WRONGALD

VOTE BILL

NOBODY-LIKES GETTING BILLS!

VOTE RONALD

If you vote for me, um, I'll do my best to...um, take care of you. Er, what you need.

And, um, make the Jedi Academy even better. Um.

Thanks.

clap
clap

clap

I'd like to thank my opponents. And I'd like to thank all of you.

Ladies and Gentlemen, this election is about choice. Your choice.

I hope today, you'll choose integrity. I hope you'll choose commitment. I hope you'll choose excellence.

I hope you'll choose me. Thank you!

CLAP
CLAP
CLAP
CLAP
CLAP
CLAP CLAP CLAP
CLAP CLAP CLAP CLAP

Wow, that was a good speech, huh?

Well, why don't you just vote for him, then?

clap clap
clap clap

clap

HEPTADAY

I'm really happy the student council elections are over, because it ended up being a lot of work just to make my friend mad at me. I was actually having fun making posters for Bill, coming up with slogans and drawing them. But then Ronald asked me to make posters for him. I was going to say no but he kept asking and saying how good my posters were and finally I just agreed to make some for him. Pretty soon Pasha asked if I'd made enough posters, and pointed to the hallway. I guess I didn't realize I made so many.

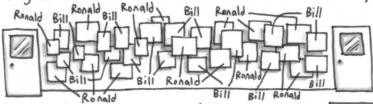

I felt pretty good, and everyone seemed to like the posters a lot, but then Bill started acting funny, like he didn't want to hang around with me. I guess he felt betrayed because I made posters for Ronald, and so I was kicking myself for doing that. Especially because half the time, Ronald was just telling me what to do and I didn't get to be very creative. But Cyrus and Cronah did talk to me and weren't as mean as usual. They kept saying to me, "You're voting for Ronald, right?" and I just sort of half nodded and didn't say anything because of course I was going to vote for Bill. Later, Pasha, Egon, and I got together to work on our math homework. Math seems really complicated sometimes but I try to remind myself that really it's all just counting. Then counting seems really complicated. Like, $x^2 - 12x + 27 = 0$

You can't do that on your fingers. Bill is good at math, but when I asked if he wanted to work with us, he said he needed to finish his history homework, which could've been true, but I feel like he's upset with me about something.

QUADDAY

I don't know why it took so long
for the student council ballots to
get counted, but we found out today
Bill didn't get elected. And even though
I voted for him, Bill is ~~defrnitly~~
definitely mad at me.

I shouldn't have made all of
those posters for Ronald!

JEDI ACADEMY STUDENT
COUNCIL MEETING

A Special Report for the
Padawan Observer
By Roan Novachez

1605 I officially call this meeting to order.

V.P. Silva, present.

Secretary Mary, present.

1606 I introduce a motion to congratulate myself on re-election.

1607 Oh, yeah, and congratulations to you guys, too.

1608 First order of business: Choose a theme for the dance.

Valentine Dance? Space Travel? The Ocean? Ewok Music?

Comics? Puppets? Zombies? Soccer? The Force?

1615 (Everyone is still thinking.)

1625 How about lightsabers?

Objection! It's been done before. I call for a vote.

All for? Two to one...

THE PADAWAN OBSERVER

VOL. MXII #8

1626 Who should organize the dance?

I will.

1628 The vote is 3-0 for Roan to make posters.

Gaiana and Carter wanted to help. Roan, will you make up some posters?

1637 Second order of business: Pick a fundraiser for the lightsaber Fencing Tournament.

1640 How about a craft and bake sale?

Sounds good.

1642 Third order of business: Silva had to go to the bathroom.

1650 Fourth order of business: Is ten minutes between classes enough time?

No. Not really. I agree.

1655 I move that we ask Master Yoda for fifteen minutes between classes.

1656

No.

Heh Heh!

1658 I hereby adjourn this student council meeting.

Should we wake Roan up?

zzzz

THE PADAWAN OBSERVER

VOL. MXII #8

How to talk to RW-22

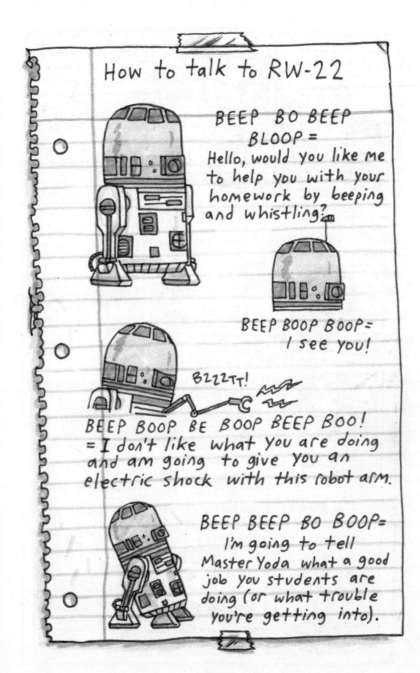

BEEP BO BEEP BLOOP =
Hello, would you like me to help you with your homework by beeping and whistling?

BEEP BOOP BOOP =
I see you!

BZZZTT!

BEEP BOOP BE BOOP BEEP BOO!
= I don't like what you are doing and am going to give you an electric shock with this robot arm.

BEEP BEEP BO BOOP =
I'm going to tell Master Yoda what a good job you students are doing (or what trouble you're getting into).

Don't pay attention to them, Silva!

They're just trying to make themselves feel better about themselves.

Thanks, guys.

Heh heh.

You guys shouldn't give Silva such a hard time...

Roan, Roan, Roan...

♪Roan, Roan, Roan♪ your ♪ boat, ♪ gently down the ♪ stream... ♪

Ha!

Ha ha ha!

Hey Ro-

Thanks for sending me copies of The Padawan Observer. It's cool that you've got your own comic strip. We don't even have comics in the Pilot Academy school paper. I hope you're sending copies of your comics to Mom and Dad, too!

Speaking of Mom and Dad, DON'T tell them but I started dating a girl here - she's a flight mechanic. Her name is Enowyn - here, I'll draw a picture of her:

Okay, I'll leave the drawing to you, I guess. I know you've made some good friends there, but what about a date for the school dance? Don't worry if you don't, just curious! Good luck on your midterms!   -DAV

P.S. Maybe when you're home for break you can show me how you use the Force — by cleaning up my room?

Man, this homework is tough.

Tell me about it.

It's not nearly as much fun as lightsaber construction, even if Mr. Garfield teaches that.

Yeah.

What'd you get for the answer to Number Seven?

"Telepathy" is the ability to sense someone else's thoughts. What did you get?

What? My answer was three hundred and fourteen.

Huh?

Wait... are you working on the assignment for History of Jedi Skills?

No, I'm doing algebra.

Oh, no, we have algebra homework, too?

It's going to be a LONG night.

PENTADAY

This week I spent a lot of time working on getting ready for the dance. Mary is in charge, and Gaiana, Carter, and I are all helping out. We spent a few afternoons just working on posters. I seem to make a lot of posters here, so maybe if I can't get into Pilot Academy, I could make posters for a living, because I'm not sure I'm cut out to be a Jedi. Everyone else seems to have a handle on it... Pasha can do a lot with the Force. Cyrus is super athletic -- last week he had four of us line up and then he leapt over us. Although, we are the four shortest kids in class. Egon is calm and focused.

Tegan has a lot of control and leadership. Gaiana is compassionate. I guess I can draw, but I don't know what that has to do with being a Jedi? At least the other kids here are pretty cool to hang out with. After we finished the last posters, Carter suggested we should get some dinner together, but the cafeteria was already closed. We went out for pizza. It was okay, but not as good as the twin sun-baked pizza Mom Makes back on Tatooine, which is the BEST. Anyway, I stayed up too late, so I had a hard time waking up. I must have turned my alarm off instead of hitting the snooze button, so I barely made it to class on time.

Ee Choya! Danvay!

That's your alarm clock, Ewok Pilot.

84

Roan, aren't you going to dance? I think you have to if you're on the committee, right?

Well, I... don't really know how.

It's easy! Watch, you just listen to the music...

And move your arms and legs!

Snicker!

Ha!

Don't worry about how you look. EVERYONE looks a little silly when they're dancing!

OKAY, WE'RE GOING TO SLOW THINGS DOWN NOW FOR A COUPLES DANCE.

85

MONODAY

I've had a really hard time falling asleep the past few days, I don't know why. At first I thought maybe I drank too much fizzy at the dance, but that doesn't explain the next couple nights. I do feel ~~nervus~~ nervous, I guess. I'm still not very good at lifting with the Force, but I'm trying. I can pick up books now-- well, A book. One book at a time. And only small paperbacks. Not any big hardcovers. Yoda keeps telling me that I need to stop trying, but that makes no sense at all. Cyrus was being a jerk about it in class today, too.

> Try not, Roan. Do. Or do not!

DUODAY

I managed to finish my research paper on early Mandalorian Sculpture a few days before it was due, and Librarian Lackbar gave me an "A".
I already took my ~~mide~~ midterm test in Mrs. Pilton's class. She smiles a lot, but I'm not sure if we do well because she's so positive, or if she's just happy because we're a good class. I only have one test left: Basic Lifting with the Force. I've learned that when Yoda laughs it's usually a good thing, so hopefully he's in a good mood, and laughs a lot.

STUDENT: ROAN NOVACHEZ		
LEVEL: PADAWAN	SEMESTER: ONE	
HOMEROOM: MASTER YODA		
REPORT CARD		

CLASS	NOTES	GRADE
BASIC LIFTING WITH THE FORCE (MASTER YODA)	Behind classmates, Roan is. Stop trying, he needs to, and just do.	D+
GALACTIC HISTORY (MRS. PILTON)	Excellent. Enjoyed use of illustrations in research papers.	a
ALGEBRA (MRS. PILTON)	Very good use of multiplication.	B+
SCIENCE (PRINCIPAL MAR)	GOOD WORK, EXCEPT FOR SCIENCE FAIR PROJECT.	B
ARTS AND LITERATURE (LIBRARIAN LACKBAR)	Roan has great reading comprehension and aesthetic taste.	A
INTRO. TO LIGHTSABER CONSTRUCTION (MR. GARFIELD)	GOOD, BUT COULD USE MORE CREATIVITY IN MAKING LIGHTSABER.	A-
PHYSICAL EDUCATION (KITMUM)		🙁

94

HOW YODA WILL PROBABLY SPEND HIS SPRING BREAK

laughing to himself about something

Heh heh!

oops! Not weeds, these are, hm?

weeding the garden

Hmmmm.

PHILOSOPHY AND DIALECTICS OF JEDI PRACTICE VOLUME 38

Catching up on reading

Getting a tan at the beach

Mmmmm, delicious, this is.

Making soup

QUADDAY

Home feels weird. I can't believe I made it through half a year of Jedi Academy. I don't feel like I'm any closer to being a Jedi, though. And I couldn't be further from being a pilot. The last two issues of Starfighter Quarterly are here, and I don't even recognize any of the spaceships. I went to the Jedi Temple Library a few times to read up on new spaceships but every time I did, I got trapped by Librarian Lackbar, who wanted to talk and talk and I'd end up listening to her for an hour without actually reading anything. The other weird thing about home is Dav. Specifically, his mustache. I think it's pretty funny. Mom keeps saying how handsome Dav is, though. Ollie is a lot different, too. He's talking a lot more. Plus, even though I can't really lift much with the Force, Ollie is really impressed by it!

Do you want to know about medical frigates?

What about Blockade Runners?

What?

Watch, Ro!

I'm using Force, too!

It must be nice to be Ollie's age. You don't have to worry about school or anything and everyone pays attention to you and feeds you and all you do is play and look at comic books. You just don't get to stay up very late, which is what Dav and I have been doing (except one night when he had to call his GIRLFRIEND).

So, Roan, what's the deal with Gaiana?

What do you mean?

Well you've been talking about her A LOT.

I have?

Dad has been home, too, and he asked me a lot about Jedi Academy. But he also talks to Dav about pilot stuff and that's when I feel left out again. I can't even talk to Reg and Jax. I've known them since we were babies, and now we have nothing in common. Is it weird that I'm actually looking forward to break ending and going back to school?

Blah Blah Blah Blah Blah Blah Blah Blah

Blah Blah Blah Blah Blah Blah

Oh wait, now the timer is too short...

The most exciting thing to happen on spring break: Dad trying to set up the holocamera for a family photo

holomail

FROM: pashawan
TO: roan_pilot17
SUBJECT: hey roan!

OPTIONS
◁ REPLY
▷ FORWARD
□ PRINT
○ POST TO HOLOBOOK

hey roan!

Thanks for the tip, I did go to the ice planet Hoth and had a ton of fun. I didn't see any wampas, though. How has your break been? Did you go anywhere exciting?

Don't let your brother get to you about Gaiana, I know you're just friends. For now, anyway, right? Sorry, I couldn't resist! =)

See you back at Academy,

Pasha

P.S. everyone is going to post pictures from break to share, make sure you post one of your adventures!

[view post]

STUDENT: ROAN NOVACHEZ

LEVEL: PADAWAN | SEMESTER: TWO

HOMEROOM: MASTER YODA

CLASS SCHEDULE

0730-0850: USING THE FORCE 101
MASTER YODA WILL CONTINUE TO TRAIN STUDENTS IN USING THE FORCE TO LIFT BIGGER AND BIGGER THINGS.

0900-0950: PRINCIPLES OF THE FORCE
MASTER YODA WILL LECTURE ON VARIOUS ASPECTS OF THE FORCE AND ITS PHILOSOPHY.

1000-1050: MATHEMATICS OF PHYSICS
MRS. PILTON WILL TEACH THE STUDENTS MATH EQUATIONS GOVERNING THE LAWS OF PHYSICS, AS WELL AS HOW TO OVERCOME THOSE LAWS.

1100-1150: BIOLOGY OF NON-HUMAN SPECIES
PRINCIPAL MAR WILL TEACH STUDENTS ABOUT KNOWN LIFE-FORMS FROM ACROSS THE GALAXY. INCLUDES TRIPS TO THE ZOO AND THE FIELD MUSEUM.

1200-1300: LUNCH BREAK

1300-1350: EARLY MANDALORIAN POETRY
STUDENTS WILL STUDY THIS ANCIENT CULTURE'S POETRY, AND WRITE THEIR OWN UNDER LIBRARIAN LACKBAR'S GUIDANCE.

1400-1450: PHYSICAL EDUCATION
KITMUM WILL LEAD STUDENTS THROUGH TRADITIONAL JEDI TRAINING EXERCISES.

1500-1550: ADVANCED LIGHTSABER DUELING
MR. GARFIELD WILL SHOW STUDENTS KEY TECHNIQUES FOR DUELING WITH LIGHTSABERS.

QUADDAY

The first thing I thought when I got back to Jedi Academy after spring break was "it's good to be home," which is odd, because I just came from my home. Although I did see a starfighter patrol on my way to Coruscant and felt a little ~~disapointed~~ disappointed. But by the time we landed I was glad to see my friends. Anyway, Pasha asked me if I was trying to run into Gaiana on purpose, because I seemed to be wandering around her dorm a lot, but really

cool air currents

Gaiana's Dorm

More shade

after being on Tatooine for a week I just needed to cool off, and besides how would I know if Gaiana was around? But then I realized maybe Pasha is right and I guess I DO like Gaiana. A little. I can't say anything anyway, because I'm sure she just likes me as a friend.

Pasha and Egon have been practicing for the Lightsaber Fencing Tournament and so I've gone to a couple of the practice sessions but it seems like nobody knows very much about what they're doing. Everybody just kind of jumps around and swings their lightsabers back and forth. They say they've actually fenced before, so maybe I'm wrong. I asked Pasha and he said he'll give me some tips.

All the warm and fuzzy feelings about being back only lasted until my first "Using the Force 101" class. We're all still getting used to waking YAWN up for class after break, so I hope Yoda doesn't — just really tired! think we're bored in class. Yoda did have a talk with me. He's pretty encouraging, so he still has faith in me.

Do it, you can!

He is seven hundred years older than me, so maybe he knows what he's talking about. But what if I get another "D"? Will they send me back to Tatooine? What if they realize I'm really not cut out to be a Jedi?

...And so, the Robotics Club would like to introduce our new protocol droid, T-P30.

clap clap clap clap clap clap clap clap clap clap clap clap clap

Thank you, Master Bill.

It is a pleasure to meet you all!

Let me begin by telling you a little bit about myself...

...and so just ten years after being manufactured, I went to Ossus, where blah blah blah and then I spent two weeks analyzing dialects of blah blah blah after which I spent the next ten years learning two million languages, including Jawa, Geonosian, Togruti, bantha mating calls, blah blah blah blah blah blah blah blah blah blah blah blah blah blah

ZZZZZZZZZZZZZZZZZZZ

Oh, dear.

SNORE

LIGHTSABER FENCING TOURNAMENT

TRYOUTS NEXT WEEK!

FIVE POSITIONS AVAILABLE FOR EACH SQUAD. SQUAD A WILL BE COACHED BY MASTER YODA. SQUAD B WILL BE COACHED BY MR. GARFIELD. SQUAD C WILL SIT IN THE BLEACHERS AND CHEER FOR EVERYONE. WATCH OUT FOR SPARKS, THOUGH!

DON'T FORGET TO BRING YOUR LIGHTSABER

HEXADAY AT 1600 IN THE GYM

109

HEXADAY

Pasha, Egon, and I have been practicing for the Lightsaber Fencing Tournament. In tryouts you don't fence anyone, you just jump around and show you can swing your lightsaber the right way. Since I can't be a star pilot, this is about the most fun I can have. I've gotten a lot better at jumping around while holding my lightsaber, even when it's not off. It's not so scary when you do it while using the Force (or, at least for me, feeling the Force). I did learn not to practice inside. I came into the dorm after practice and I don't know what I was doing, I just did some sort of flip thing and my lightsaber turned on and chopped a corner off the sofa. So now I have to sit on that side until it's fixed, which is fair. The worst part was that Yoda saw it happen. He could tell I felt bad and tried to cheer me up, although I can't tell if that's a good thing for him to say or not. Still, I think Yoda really likes me.

Not bad, you are doing, since later you started.

Mr. Garfield, though, definitely DOESN'T like me. Actually, I don't think he likes ANYONE. I'm sure he's a great Jedi or whatever, but this week he's substitute teaching for Principal Mar's class and it's been awful. Mr. G. gave us a pop quiz on the history of Xim's Empire in the Tion Cluster prior to the founding of the Galactic Republic. We tried to tell him we didn't even cover that material in class, but he said that didn't matter, we should know the history anyway. Most of us got bad grades,

But that's ancient history!

YOUR GRADE IN THIS CLASS IS ABOUT TO BE HISTORY.

OVERACHIEVERS!

but somehow Egon and Shi-Fara both got "A's", so the rest of us didn't have as much of an excuse. Pasha and I came up with a list of Dos and Don'ts for when Mr. Garfield is teaching...

DO	DON'T
- Pay VERY, VERY close attention	- Draw any attention to yourself
- Look busy	- Make any noise
- Sit up straight	- Smile (or worse, laugh!)

Hmm. Next up for lightsaber fencing tryouts...

...Roan is.

100-yard dash

cardio treadmill test

Jumping

Lightsaber accuracy

Triple Somersault

Deflecting lasers

Bew!

Bew!

Bew!

Spinning around

Very good. Thank you, Roan.

If there's a bonus for sweating, I definitely qualified!

Yuck, dude!

TRIDAY

I think I did okay at the tryouts. It was hard work, but compared to farming on Tatooine it wasn't bad. RW-22 and T-P30 were keeping track of times and everything, but T-P30 kept saying stuff

← me on Tatooine

right when people were about to go and totally distracted them a few times. Like, Silva tripped while running,

The odds of Silva running the 100-yard dash in twelve seconds are approximately four hundred and seventy thousand to one.

although he seemed relieved to be disqualified. I think Yoda was going to give him another try, but Mr. Garfield said we should all learn a lesson from Silva. →

A JEDI MUST BE ABLE TO FOCUS, AND IGNORE DISTRACTIONS.

Pasha, Egon, and I wanted to keep practicing after tryouts, so we put our money together and ordered our own training droid. It

MARKSMAN-H COMBAT REMOTE
WARNING:

floats in the air and shoots little shock lasers at you. I'm getting pretty good at deflecting lasers, I think because I want to avoid getting shocked so badly.

Gaiana, Tegan, and Shi-fara have come

over to practice
with us a few
times. Gaiana is pretty
good. I've been
trying to watch her
(because I think I
can learn from her techniques).
I think I may see if she wants to
practice more sometime next week.
We also let Cyrus borrow the droid.
He said he would just borrow it for
a couple of hours, but Pasha finally had
to go and get it after two days.
When we got it back, it was a little
dented, and one of the lasers wasn't
working. Plus there
was some sticky
gum or something
on it. Egon said
at least
it still
floats ← he figured
that was
going to happen,
but Pasha and I were surprised.
Egon said that's because we're
too nice. I still don't think being
nice is a bad thing, we just won't
let Cyrus borrow the droid again.

RW-22 won't play the slide show for my lecture...

BEEP BOOP

Does anyone know how to get him to work?

Let's see... if we fiddle with this...

Use this pen, Roan.

I think... I just...

Try hitting him on the top, Pasha.

There.

clank

Okay, class, you're all going to have to do handstands for today's lecture.

QUANTUM ELECTRO-DYNAMICS

EWOK PILOT
By Roan Novachez

Ewok Pilot, you need to start using your lasers in battle.

Plus, that was MY starfighter!

Yub Yub!

Sorry, Ewok Pilot, you're fired.

Yub?

To be continued!

HOLOSCOPE!
By Jo-Ahn

RANCOR	WAMPA	BOGA
The Force is strong in you today.	You'll only bring to class what you take with you.	I sense a great disturbance in your afternoon.
BANTHA	**NEXU**	**DEWBACK**
Today is a good day for you to hug a Wookiee.	You're doomed! Might as well stay in bed.	Watch out for droids beeping at you!
NERF	**TAUNTAUN**	**MYNOCK**
Sometimes it's easier to work as a team.	Decisive action will make you happy.	Don't worry so much, it doesn't help!
SARLACC	**ACKLAY**	**OPEE**
Use your feelings!	Don't forget to be flexible.	Today is a good day to take it easy.

121

holomail

FROM: master_yoda_642
TO: Padawan Class Group
SUBJECT: Tournament Qualifiers

OPTIONS
◀ REPLY
▶ FORWARD
▣ PRINT
● POST TO HOLOBOOK

Dear Padawan Class,

For this year's 149th annual LIGHTSABER FENCING TOURNAMENT, the student qualifiers are:

1. Pasha *
2. Cyrus *
3. Jo-Ahn
4. Egon
5. Tegan
6. Cronah
7. Gaiana
8. Shi-Fara
9. Greer
10. Roan

click here to watch holovideo of qualifying exercises

* By Team Captains [Top Two Qualifiers], squads will be chosen.

To everyone, CONGRATULATIONS! Heh heh.

-Yoda

HEPTADAY

I did it! I qualified for the Lightsaber Fencing Tournament! And my team is better, I think. Pasha is the captain of Squad A and Cyrus is captain of Squad B. Today they chose teams. Pasha took me first — I think some people were sort of surprised, because I'm maybe not the best, but Pasha's seen me practice a lot. I thought Cyrus would pick Cronah first, and I think Cronah thought so, too, because when Cyrus chose Jo-Ahn first, Cronah made this sad face. The rest of my team is Gaiana, Tegan, and Egon. Cyrus also picked Cronah, Shi-Fara, and Greer. I'm glad I'm not on Cyrus's team, even if he does have a cool hood and everything. Cronah gave me a dirty look afterward, so I can't imagine being on a team with him. I can't believe I almost asked him to be my lab partner the first week of class! That would've been a disaster. The whole Lightsaber Fencing Tournament

Should we work on our project?

No! I'm too busy making grumpy faces.

has taken up a lot of time, though. I'm not quite finished with my next few Ewok Pilot comics. Since half the newspaper staff is in the Fencing Tournament,

I bet the next issue will be a little late, anyway. Sometimes it all seems kind of overwhelming, because there's always so much to do, but I want to stay busy. It keeps me from thinking about Pilot Academy too much. Or maybe I'm thinking less about becoming a pilot anyway... it's hard to imagine leaving my friends here now. Tonight Pasha invited all of his squad to get together for a celebration dinner. Gaiana asked me to pick her up at her dorm on my way, to make sure she wasn't late. Which is odd, because she's never late.

Principles of the Force

Creatures able to resist the Force

1. Hutts
   - Jedi mind tricks don't work (maybe they're too big?)
   - can't run fast
   - <u>can</u> be lifted by Force because size does not matter

2. Toydarians
   - Jedi mind tricks don't work on them, but regular mind tricks can

3. Ysalamir
   - Create Force-resistant bubble
   - Mostly just live in trees

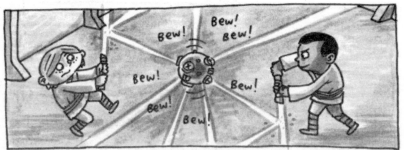

Good job, Roan... try this, too... swing down--

--you can block your opponent's lightsaber, then counterattack.

Cool!

Hey, Pasha. How's training?

Hey, Cyrus. Hey, Cronah.

Hey, Roan, I hope I get matched up against you! It'll be an easy win.

Don't be so sure, Cronah. Roan's learned a lot.

Panel 1: Oh, yeah? I just perfected three more moves!

Panel 2: Watch! — Uh, Cronah, wait —

Panel 3: Like this! Buzzzzz Click!

Panel 4: OUCH! Zap! Zap! Zap! Zap! Zap!

We were trying to warn you, the practice droid is set on automatic for detecting activated lightsabers!

See you guys later.

Remember, a Jedi should always be prepared!

I thought that was the Padawan Scouts?

Them, too!

Stuff Yoda said this week

PENTADAY

I think I'll consider the Lightsaber Fencing Tournament a victory as long as I don't throw up before it. No one else seems especially nervous. I just keep reminding myself it's only an ~~extracueutar~~ extracurricular activity, and it's not like it has anything to do with being a pilot. I'll try to do my best. And I hope I don't have to fence Cyrus because he'd probably embarrass me. I bet I'll have to fence Cronah, which will be the most annoying thing ever if he beats me.

149th ANNUAL
CORUSCANT JEDI ACADEMY
LIGHTSABER FENCING TOURNAMENT

—*○ Program of Events ○*—

INTRODUCTORY REMARKS
   by Principal Mar

EXHIBITION DUEL
   Mr. Garfield vs. (Master Yoda)

MATCH ONE *Definitely!*
   (Gaiana) (Squad A) vs. Greer (Squad B)

MATCH TWO
   Roan (Squad A) vs. (Jo-Ahn) (Squad B)   *I wonder if I'll be the only one on my team to lose?!*

MATCH THREE
   (Egon) (Squad A) vs. Shi-Fara (Squad B)

MATCH FOUR   *Sorry Shi-Fara!*
   (Tegan) (Squad A) vs. Cronah (Squad B)

MATCH FIVE *this one will be close*
   (Pasha) (Squad A) vs. Cyrus (Squad B)

TOURNAMENT AWARDS
   Presented by Librarian Lackbar

—*○ Reception with juice
      and cookies will ○*—
   follow the tournament

Brzkk!

PASHA!

Huh?!

~click!

Hey! Someone turned my lightsaber off!

Oh. No.

That's cheating!

I think Pasha is disqualified.

Hmmm.

Disqualified, Pasha is. Win the match, Cyrus does.

SHRINK

The Padawan Observer

EDITED BY THE STUDENTS OF JEDI ACADEMY · VOL. MXII #14

LIGHTSABER FENCING TOURNAMENT ENDS IN CONTROVERSY!

PADAWAN ROAN NOVACHEZ CAUGHT HELPING TEAM CAPTAIN CHEAT

The Annual Jedi Academy Lightsaber Tournament ended controversially as Squad A captain Pasha was disqualified after his opponent, Squad B captain Cyrus, had his lightsaber deactivated by a spectator (identified as Roan Novachez). Although Pasha was ahead two points to zero and claimed to be unaware of the interference, the judges had no choice but to award victory to Cyrus. As a result, Squad B, coached by Mr. Garfield, won the tournament three matches to two. Master

Yoda praised all the competitors for showing excellent Jedi abilities. Librarian Lackbar was then interrupted during the award ceremony by student council President Ronald, who insisted on presenting Cyrus with a homemade "President's Trophy" and making us all sit through a ten-minute speech.

FULL TOURNAMENT RESULTS:

EXHIBITION: Master Yoda Def. Mr. Garfield
1. Gaiana Def. Greer (3-0)
2. Jo-Ahn Def. Roan (3-1)
3. Egon Def. Shi-Fara (3-2)
4. Cronah Def. Tegan (3-2)
5. Cyrus Def. Pasha (DQ)
SQUAD B WINS 3-2.

HEPTADAY

So, it's true. I did cheat. But it's TOTALLY NOT how everyone is making it look. First, Pasha really had no idea, and he's completely innocent. He didn't deserve to get disqualified. I think he probably would've won his match, too, even if he was going to lose one round. And I admitted right away that it was me. How could anyone think I did it on purpose? Everyone knows how bad I am at using the Force. At least it didn't happen in class, because I'd probably get expelled. I'm pretty sure Yoda is disappointed even if he does sound pretty positive. Pasha and the team must want to kill me. That's why I've decided to avoid everyone. I plan to just stay hidden until school is over.

Mere numbers, success is not.

More to winning than how game ends, there is.

← coached losing team

Oh, man, everyone must think I'm a loser...

KNOCK KNOCK KNOCK

Roan?

Hm, he must not be here?

Maybe I can find a place to hide, and just study more...

If I mess the final up, I'll get kicked out for sure...

I *AM* going to end up at Plant School.

Oh, no, it's Pasha!

TRIDAY

I thought Jedi Academy would be a waste
of time, but it turned out to be great...
at least, it was until last week.
I don't know why anyone would want
to stay friends with me now, because
they all think I'm a cheater, even
though I'm not. Now I have to take
this final exam, which I'm totally
going to fail, because I don't even
know how to use the Force the
right way. I thought even though I
didn't get into Pilot School, at least
I wouldn't have to go to Plant School.
That's where I'll end up after this
exam. I've been trying to lift
things with the Force all year, but
I might as well give up trying. I
hope everyone doesn't laugh at
me too much when I fail this
test. This is the worst. I don't
even feel like drawing right now.

142

Your turn, it is, Roan, hm?

My turn to fail...

After this it's off to Plant School.

Well, that's it.

I guess I can stop trying so hard.

Whoa!

What?

Why is everyone looking at me like that?

Roan...look behind you!

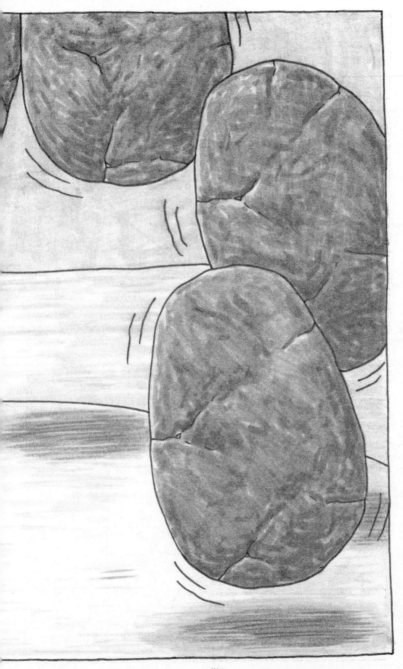

Everyone is looking at me differently...

...and for once, it's not because I messed something up! All my work finally paid off.

Hmmm... Impressive, that was!

Thanks, Master Yoda!

Right about you, I was, hm? Powerful Jedi you may become.

Hm. Hesitation, I sense in you?

uh

Not a Jedi, you wish to become, hm?

Oh, er, well...

Hm...

Come back next year, I think you will.

Well, I guess I could try one more year...

Heh Heh Heh!

STUDENT: ROAN NOVACHEZ		
LEVEL: PADAWAN	SEMESTER: TWO	
HOMEROOM: MASTER YODA		

REPORT CARD

CLASS	NOTES	GRADE
USING THE FORCE 101 (MASTER YODA)	Impressive. Most impressive.	A+
PRINCIPLES OF THE FORCE (MASTER YODA)	Good - but Roan asked too many questions during meditation.	B+
MATHEMATICS OF PHYSICS (MRS. PILTON)	Despite drawing during lectures, Roan did well in solving equations.	a-
BIOLOGY OF NON-HUMAN SPECIES (PRINCIPAL MAR)	ROAN HAS A NATURAL GRASP OF ALIEN ANATOMY.	A-
EARLY MANDALORIAN POETRY (LIBRARIAN LACKBAR)	Good interpretations, and did very well with his own rhymes.	A
PHYSICAL EDUCATION (KITMUM)		☺
ADVANCED LIGHTSABER DUELING (MR. GARFIELD)	NOT BAD FOR A BEGINNER.	B-

MOST LIKELY TO BE ON HOLOTELEVISION	MOST LIKELY TO GO BALD	MOST LIKELY TO BE A GALACTIC SENATOR
BEST SPORT	MOST ATHLETIC	SMARTEST
MOST LIKELY TO BEEP CONSTANTLY	MOST CREATIVE	BEST DRESSED

MOST NERVOUS	MOST LIKELY TO SUCCEED	BEST DANCER
PRETTIEST RODIAN	BEST HAND-EYE COORDINATION	CALMEST UNDER PRESSURE
BEST SENSE OF HUMOR	MOST LIKELY TO BECOME A JEDI	BEST HAIR

DUODAY

So, I made it through an entire year at Jedi Academy... I finally got the hang of things, even if it took the whole time. Everyone seems to think of me as part of the school, and I feel like I belong... and now I have to go home. I was almost hoping Yoda would tell me to stay for summer school to make up for my "D+" the first semester, but he decided my final exam balanced it out. Besides, I'd be the only one here, which would be no fun. Last night was the Jedi Academy Good-bye Dinner. We all signed each other's yearbooks— even Cronah signed mine, although it was just a bad joke. A lot of people asked me to draw Ewok Pilot in their books. I was going to draw me and Gaiana dancing in hers,

but I chickened out, because I was worried other people might see it. I'm going to miss hanging out with her this summer. And Pasha. Tatooine is going to feel even MORE boring without them.

Yoda seemed a little emotional. I'm going to miss him, too. Especially now that I can finally understand what he's saying. Most of the time. I think he likes us. After the final exam, though, he's been pulling me aside even more than usual, and saying cryptic things. Not like Mr. Garfield, who spent most of the dinner standing near the wall kind of in the shadows. He made a "Harumph" sound when he found out I'd be coming back next year, so I think he still has it out for me.

Proud of you, I am.

A good class, you are.

I'M WATCHING YOU!

Another thing I'll miss is RW-22 beeping. At first, I had this constant nagging feeling that the smoke alarm battery needed to be replaced or a space truck was backing up. Now when I don't hear beeping, it feels too quiet. I'm definitely going to draw more comics this summer. Maybe I'll make my own comic book to send to everyone. Enough writing, I fly home tomorrow, and I still need to pack!

BEEP BOOP BLEEP

153

I talked to my friend at Pilot Academy. He's going to see if you can apply for a transfer, if you want to try...

Oh, thanks, Dad! But... I think maybe I'll stay at Jedi Academy, actually...

Really? That's great!

Ah, home!

Roan, this letter was waiting for you... do you know someone named "Gaiana"?

Do you and Pasha want to go on the Corellian Run with me when he visits?

Roan, look! I'm using the Force!

Ro, can I see your lightsaber?

THE END (of the school year)

157

START YOUR OWN JOURNAL!

First, find a blank sketchbook or journal to use! Lined or unlined paper will both work.

*have fun!

Draw some comics! Even if you *think* you can't draw, go ahead! It's still fun to draw, and it's YOUR journal!

write about what happened to you today

put in some photos of you and your friends

use different kinds of pens and colors!

*write at least ten words a day

Include some of your classwork that you like or did well on

cut out and tape or paste in magazine articles, newspaper clippings — what's your favorite TV show, movie, or book? What's something that happened in the news?

Write down your most embarrassing moments — they'll actually become LESS embarrassing and funnier!

Jeffrey Brown is a cartoonist and author of the bestselling **DARTH VADER AND SON** and its sequel **VADER'S LITTLE PRINCESS**. He lives in Chicago with his wife and two sons. Despite his best efforts, Jeffrey has never been able to use the Force, and so had to go to a normal middle school and never became a Jedi. He still loves StarWars.

P.O. Box 120 Deerfield IL 60015-0120 USA